# AND THE WICKED

Created by

**JIM DAVIS**

**Written by Michael Teitelbaum**
**Designed and Illustrated**
**by Mike Fentz**

"Wake up!" Jon Arbuckle shouted as he bounded down the stairs from his bedroom and dashed into the living room. "Today's the big day!"

Garfield and Odie were sprawled on the living room rug. Odie instantly sprang to his feet and trotted happily over to Jon, leaving a fresh puddle of dog drool on the carpet where he had been resting.

Garfield, on the other hand, opened his eyelids halfway, scratched himself lazily, and smirked. "What big day?" he wondered. "The day your

3

favorite plaid pants come back from the cleaners to join your twelve other pairs of plaid pants?"

"I'm taking you to the Medieval Festival!" Jon said excitedly.

"Sounds like there might be some walking and fresh air involved," Garfield mumbled, rolling over and scratching his other side. "Count me out."

"The festival is a re-creation of the time of King Arthur, Sir Lancelot, Sir Galahad, and the Knights of the Round Table," Jon explained.

"Table?" Garfield repeated, his ears perking up for the first time. "Now that's a word I like. Tables often have food on them. Maybe this won't be so bad, after all."

"We'll see a castle, storytellers, jugglers, and people dressed up in the clothes they wore back then," Jon continued.

"You mean there are people who have clothes older than yours?" Garfield asked in amazement.

"And my favorite part," Jon said happily, "is the jousting tournaments. Two knights in armor charge at each other on horseback. They use long jousting poles to try to knock each other off their horses."

"Big deal," Garfield muttered. "Your breath could knock someone over any day of the week."

"Come on, you two," Jon urged, hustling his pets toward the front door. "We don't want to be late."

"Oh, no," Garfield said, grabbing onto the carpet with his front claws as Jon tried to pull him from the house. "We wouldn't want to be late to see a couple of guys in tin cans riding big, smelly animals."

"Garfield!" Jon shouted.

"Okay, fine!" Garfield whined as he let go of the carpet. "Like it or not, King Awkward, Sir Lunch-A-Lot, and Sir Drool-Face are off to the fair!"

The Medieval Festival fairgrounds were a colorful, noisy jumble of people and activity. Flags waved from the tops of large red and yellow tents. Trumpets blared, announcing each event. Jugglers tossed brightly colored balls high into

the air. A crowd of people listened to a storyteller's tale of wizards and magic. Nearby, a minstrel sang of a brave knight who battled two fire-breathing dragons to rescue a beautiful princess.

Jon, Garfield, and Odie strolled up and down the fairgrounds. Jon's eyes opened wide in amazement, and a big

smile spread across his face. Odie's head spun left, then right, trying to take in all the colors and movement and excitement.

Garfield was totally bored. "If I wanted to spend the day in a place that was loud, busy, and filled with clashing colors, I could have just curled up in Jon's closet," the fat cat said. He gazed around at the merriment and music. "There's got to be a food stand here somewhere. I wonder if there's such a thing as mutton lasagna."

A young woman dressed in a long flowing robe, wearing the crown of a princess, rushed over to Jon. "Good day, handsome sir," she said sweetly.

"Whom could she be talking to?" Garfield wondered. "It couldn't possibly be Jon!"

"I am Princess Goodflower," the

woman explained. "And I bring good news. A grand puppet show is about to begin in yonder tent." The princess pointed to a small yellow tent nearby.

"Wow, puppets!" Jon exclaimed. "Cool! Just as long as I'm not late for the big jousting tournament!"

"Oh, you won't be, good sir," the princess assured Jon. "But hurry now, the show is about to begin!"

"Did you hear that, guys?" Jon said, turning to the pets. "Puppets! It'll be fun. Come on."

"Big fat hairy deal . . ." Garfield moaned as he followed Jon and Odie to the show tent. "Last time I checked, you couldn't eat puppets, right? So where's the fun?"

Inside the tent, the puppet show was underway. On a small stage, in front of a cheering audience, one puppet was dressed up like a princess and another wore a knight's armor. The knight came riding in on a horse and promptly fell off, to the delight and laughter of the audience. The princess screamed at the knight, who screamed back, then they began whacking each other. Soon the whole set collapsed around them. As the curtain fell, the two puppets could still be heard arguing.

"Now *that's* funny!" Jon said as he leaped to his feet and applauded wildly.

"Does that mean it's okay for me to do all that stuff to Odie?" Garfield asked hopefully.

Just then, the back flap of the tent flew open, and in walked a man carrying a long trumpet. A blue banner with a picture of two knights jousting hung from the trumpet.

The man blew a few blasts on the

trumpet. After everyone in the small tent had recovered from the loud noise, the man spoke. "Hear ye! Hear ye! The great jousting tournament is about to begin," he said. "Come ye then, one and all, to the jousting field!"

"Oh boy!" Jon cried. "This is my favorite part!"

"My favorite part is when we go home, eat for four hours, then nap for another twelve," Garfield muttered. "When can we do that?"

The crowd, including Jon and his pets, made their way to the jousting field. Two men clad in shining armor sat atop a pair of huge horses. The snorting animals stood at opposite sides of the field, ready to fight. One knight's armor was all silver. The other knight had a bright red dragon painted on his shield.

The princess who had invited Jon

to the puppet show sat high up on a platform, off to the side of the field, midway between the two knights. She held out a white scarf. "When this scarf reaches the ground, you may begin," the princess announced. Then she released the scarf, which drifted gently to the ground.

The knights took off as if they had been shot from cannons. With their

long jousting lances pointed straight
ahead, they urged their mighty horses
on. Dust clouds trailed behind them as
the horses' powerful hooves pounded the
earth.

*WHAM!*

The two knights' great steel lances collided at midfield.

*CLANK! THUD!*

The red knight hit the ground and rolled to a stop. The silver knight reined in his horse, then raised his weapon in victory.

"The first contest goes to the silver knight," the princess declared from her perch high above the action. "The silver knight will now face the green knight."

"How about a 'nighty-knight, sleep tight,'" Garfield said, rolling his eyes in boredom. "That's the only knight I want to see."

Before the next contest began, Garfield's hunger got the better of him. "There's got to be something to eat around here," he whispered to Odie. "These brave knights couldn't have jousted and rescued princesses and fought fire-breathing dragons on empty stomachs! Let's go joust with some medieval pizza!"

As the green and silver knights prepared to joust, Garfield and Odie slipped away. Jon was so caught up in the action, he never saw them leaving.

The two pets wandered all over the fairgrounds searching for food. They eventually came to an ancient-looking castle surrounded by a moat. The tall stone structure rose into the sky, looking as if it had just popped out of a fairy tale.

"Maybe there's food in there," Garfield said, pointing to the castle's huge wooden front door.

Odie followed as Garfield strolled across the drawbridge that had been lowered over the moat.

Suddenly the massive door flew open, and out charged a dozen knights

on horseback, racing at full speed. Garfield and Odie froze in fear. In a few seconds they would be squished into pet pancakes by the onrushing hooves.

There was only one thing to do.

"JUMP!" Garfield shouted. He grabbed Odie's paw and leaped off the drawbridge, pulling the clueless canine with him.

# 3

*SPLASH! SPLOOSH!*

The two pets plunged into the cold water of the moat.

Garfield struggled back to the surface, gasping for breath. "I hate swimming!" he gurgled through the stream of water pouring from his mouth. "It's too much like bathing!"

Odie, on the other hand, like most dogs, was an excellent swimmer. He dog paddled (what else?) to shore, planted his paws firmly on the ground, then leaned over and plucked Garfield from the water with his mouth.

"Yuck!" Garfield yelled once he was safely on dry land, shaking the water from his fur. "Now I also have dog slobber on me!"

He looked around for the knights on horseback, prepared to give them a piece of his mind, but they were nowhere to be seen. "Did you get the license plate number of those horses, Odie?"

Odie handed Garfield a crumpled, rusty license plate he had found on the murky bottom of the moat. It read, "#1 KNIGHT."

Garfield sighed and tossed the plate away. Then he looked up at the castle. "We're still no closer to lasagna," he complained.

"At last, help has arrived!" said a squeaky voice coming from the ground next to Garfield's left leg.

Looking toward the sound, Garfield saw something that stunned him. There stood a tiny cat, no bigger than a mouse. Garfield bent down and looked the cat right in its teeny eyes. "You can take off the cat costume, Mouse," he whispered. "Halloween's over."

An angry expression came over the miniature cat's face. He crossed his arms in front of his chest, then stuck his nose into the air. "And just what are you dressed up as?" he asked, poking Garfield's belly with a tiny finger. "A big orange bowling ball with legs? For your information, I happen to be the king's loyal pet. My name is Hairball, and I am the royal cat of this castle."

Garfield burst into laughter. Odie eyed the odd little creature curiously.

"And what exactly is so funny?" Hairball demanded.

"Oh, nothing," Garfield answered. "I come across five-inch-tall cats who think they belong to a king every day. Well, this has been fun, but we've got to get back to the Medieval Festival."

"The what?" Hairball asked.

"You know, the big show with

knights and puppets and princesses," Garfield replied.

"You're not at any show," Hairball explained. "You are in the kingdom of Fanta-see-a."

"Right," Garfield said, looking at Odie. He rolled his eyes and pointed down at Hairball. "I suppose this is a magical kingdom filled with unicorns, fairies, and three-headed, fire-breathing dragons," he added sarcastically.

"Well, the fire-breathing dragons have only two heads," Hairball replied.

"But otherwise, you are quite correct."

Garfield heard a group of high-pitched voices giggling softly behind him. He spun around and saw ten little fairies, each about an inch tall, flying up near his head. They looked like small shimmering butterflies with sparkling, delicate wings. A blue glow surrounded each fairy. Garfield's jaw dropped open in amazement. The fairies giggled once more, then vanished from sight.

Garfield next heard the sound of galloping hooves nearby. He looked toward the sound, expecting to see another annoying knight on horseback. Instead, he saw a unicorn. The beautiful white creature galloped gracefully, its silver horn gleaming in the bright sunlight.

Suddenly, a mighty roar filled the sky. The frightened unicorn bolted for

25

the safety of the nearby woods. Looking up, Garfield saw a two-headed dragon flying through the air. Flames shot from both of its mouths. The dragon circled once, then flew off into the clouds.

"W-W-Well, this p-place is really terrific,"

Garfield stammered, backing away slowly. "I don't know how we got here. But I just remembered I left a large lasagna with extra cheese in the oven back in my world. You know, the one where there are no fairies, unicorns, or dragons. And I hate it when the cheese turns all brown. So I've got to go home. Come on, Odie, we're leaving."

"But you can't leave," Hairball reminded Garfield. "You don't know how you got here. That means you don't know how to get back to your world. I'm the only one who can tell you how to get home."

"Great!" replied Garfield. "Then we've found the right five-inch-tall cat. How do we do it?"

"I'm not telling you," Hairball said, crossing his arms over his chest. "Not until you help me."

"Okay, Shorty, help you do what?" Garfield asked impatiently. "Get some cat food off the top shelf?"

"Not exactly," Hairball answered. "You're going to help me rescue my king from the evil clutches of a wicked wizard!"

Odie followed Garfield with his eyes as the fat cat fainted and crashed to the ground.

When Garfield recovered, he and Odie listened in amazement as Hairball told his story.

"My master, good King Butterball, rules Fanta-see-a," the tiny cat began. "He is fair and good to his people. We lived happily in this castle until Magico, the wicked wizard, kidnapped the king. Magico took him to his creepy fortress. He is holding the king because he wants to take over the entire kingdom!

"I tried to stop Magico from taking King Butterball, but he cast a spell on me. He shrunk me down to mouse size.

You and the drooling dog must help me free the king and save Fanta-see-a."

"Don't you have brave knights in shining armor to do this sort of work?" Garfield asked.

"Two days ago, the king's bravest knights set off for Magico's fortress," Hairball explained. "They never came back. I fear the worst."

"You know," said Garfield, "I'm not a real big fan of the worst. I prefer happy endings. So maybe you need to find another cat to help you on your nice little rescue mission."

"And how will you get home?" Hairball asked.

"Good point," muttered Garfield, scratching his head. "I know I'm going to hate myself for saying this, but let's go rescue the king!"

Hairball climbed up onto Odie's

back, and the threesome set out for Magico's spooky fortress. As they got closer, the bright blue sky faded to gray, then darkened to black. The evil of Magico's powers reached out from his lair and hung over the countryside.

It took most of that day to reach the fortress. As the sky turned gloomier, Garfield's mood followed right along. "Don't you Fanta-see-a folks believe in restaurants?" he asked crankily about every ten minutes. "We haven't passed one pizza place. And you call yourself a kingdom! What about motels? There hasn't been one single sign that says 'Vacancy. Nice comfy place to take a nap!'"

"Will you stop whining!" Hairball cried.

"NO!" Garfield shot back. "And another thing. I—"

Suddenly Garfield came to a dead stop. Odie was so busy watching a small blue fairy in a nearby tree that he didn't notice. He crashed into Garfield, sending Hairball flying.

"Hey! Watch where you're going!" Hairball screamed as he scrambled back up Odie's leg.

Garfield didn't hear the pint-sized feline. He was staring straight ahead, mouth open, speechless.

A massive castle loomed before them. Its dark gray stones dripped with a disgusting green goo. Waves of black smoke hung over the place. A shiver ran down Garfield's spine, then back up, then down once more for good measure.

"P-P-Please don't tell me that's the wizard's fortress?" Garfield stammered, his knees banging together in rhythm like two bony maracas.

"Yup, that's the wizard's fortress," Hairball replied.

"I asked you not to tell me that!" Garfield shouted, backing away slowly. "Well, I've seen enough. Sorry, pal, but it looks like that wizard dude is going to win. Sorry about your king and your kingdom, but I gotta go!"

"And where, exactly, are you going?" Hairball asked.

Garfield sighed. "Right. You know the way home, and you're not talking." He took a deep breath, stood up tall, and mustered all his courage. "There's only one thing to do, then."

Garfield dropped to his knees, clasped his hands in front of his face, and began begging. "Oh, please, oh, please, oh, *please* tell me how to get home!"

"And you call yourself a cat!" Hairball hissed. "Don't you have any dignity? This is the most disgusting display I've ever seen."

"You've never seen me alone in a pizza parlor after midnight," Garfield replied, getting back to his feet. "*That* can be a pretty disgusting sight."

"You're a coward," Hairball said.

"Yes," Garfield replied proudly. "In fact, I'm a lifetime member of the International Society of Cowards. Our last meeting was canceled because everyone was too afraid to show up."

"Follow me," ordered Hairball, leaping bravely down from Odie's back and marching forward.

"I was afraid you'd say something like that," Garfield muttered, as he trailed reluctantly behind.

As the group approached Magico's house, they were startled by a loud noise.

*ROOAARR!!*

"I hope that was just my stomach," Garfield said.

The black sky turned even darker, and smoke was everywhere. Then two more roars came from above.

*ROOAARR!! ROOAARR!!*

The three pets looked up and saw

a three-headed, fire-breathing dragon.

"I thought you said the dragons around here had two heads," Garfield whined as he looked left and right, desperately trying to find a place to hide.

"The regular ones do," Hairball answered nervously. "This must be a special beast created by one of Magico's spells."

"Well, that makes me feel *much* better!" Garfield cried as the dragon swooped down toward them.

"We're doomed!" Hairball cried. "I'm about to be turned into a tiny order of well-done cat fries!"

At the mention of food, Odie's mouth began to water. Drool dripped from his jowls, splashing onto his paw.

"I have an idea!" Garfield shouted. "Quickly, name every delicious food you can think of!" Garfield grabbed Odie's mouth and squeezed his jaws shut.

"Ice cream!" Hairball called out.

"Lasagna! Pizza! More lasagna!" Garfield added.

"Pie with ice cream! Cake with ice

cream! Tuna with ice cream!" Hairball yelled.

"Tuna with ice cream?" Garfield asked.

"Hey, back off," Hairball said. "I'm under a lot of pressure here."

As the cats listed their favorite foods, Odie's drool factor whipped into high gear. With both Garfield's hands clamped firmly around Odie's jaws, his cheeks expanded as more and more drool filled his mouth.

The dragon flew closer. It raised its three heads and opened its three mouths, then prepared to fire streams of flame that would barbecue the pets.

At the last second, Garfield pulled Odie's jaws open and turned the dog's head to face the oncoming beast. A huge stream of drool shot from Odie's mouth and splashed over the dragon's heads just as the terrible creature was about to unleash his fire-breath.

The drool not only doused the dragon's flame, it startled and confused the beast as well. It shrieked, then spun out of control. Down it plunged, splashing into the slimy green moat that encircled the fortress. Steam rose from the black water as the dragon's fire was put out for good. A thin line of gray smoke drifted from the moat as the magical creature vanished.

"You go, Odie!" Hairball shouted.

"Who ever said you were useless?" Garfield asked, patting his buddy on the head. "Oh, I guess that was me."

"Let's not celebrate yet," Hairball said, turning serious again. "We've still got to get into that horrible place."

The three pets moved quickly until they were outside the main entrance to the fortress.

"Those are odd lawn ornaments," Garfield said. He pointed to dozens of armor-clad figures that were frozen in various positions around the front of the fortress.

"Those aren't lawn ornaments!" Hairball gasped. "Those are the king's knights! Magico must have cast a spell on them."

Garfield noticed that one of the frozen knights was holding a chicken leg. "He won't miss this," he said, snatching the leg from the knight's grip and devouring it hungrily. He tossed the cleaned chicken bone over his shoulder and looked up nervously at the oozing fortress. "Besides," Garfield muttered, "everyone is entitled to a last meal!"

The trio crept quietly up to the fortress's huge front door. Garfield tried turning the large brass doorknob, but it wouldn't budge.

"No one's home. Let's go!" Garfield whispered quickly as he turned to leave.

"Not so fast, cat," Hairball said. "I've got a plan. I think I know a way to use my size to get that door open."

"What are you planning to do?" Garfield asked. "Tickle the bottom of the wizard's foot when he tries to squish you like a bug?"

"No, listen," Hairball insisted. "Lift me up to the doorknob. I think I can slip through the keyhole and unlock the door from the inside."

Hairball jumped onto Garfield's outstretched palm, and Garfield lifted the mini-cat up to the keyhole. Hairball peered inside, then climbed through.

"I'm in!" he whispered. "Give me a few seconds to unlock the door."

"Oh, take your time," Garfield whispered back. "I'm happy to stand here until I'm turned into a scared, tired, hungry, homesick statue!"

On the other side of the doorknob, Hairball slid down the smooth brass handle until he landed on the lock. But before he could unlock the door, a small, squeaky voice called up from below.

"What the heck are you supposed to be?" the voice said.

Hairball looked down and saw a mouse staring up at him from the floor. "I'm a cat," he growled angrily, revealing his tiny but sharp claws. "And when I get down there, I'll slice you into bite-sized mousy snacks."

"Are you sure you're not a mouse in a cat costume?" the mouse asked.

"I told you, I am a cat—not a mouse!" Hairball hissed back.

The mouse began giggling, and soon he was squeaking uncontrollably with whiny laughter.

"What is this, laugh at Hairball day?" the tiny cat asked with a sigh. The mouse ran off, snickering as he disappeared into a crack in the stone wall.

Hairball turned back to the lock and quickly had the door open. Garfield and Odie slipped through.

The inside of the fortress was even creepier than the outside. The same green goo that dripped from the outside walls also oozed from the inside. Garfield had the feeling they had entered a living, breathing body instead of a building. A steady stream of insects skittered across the damp stone floor. It looked like a living carpet of bugs.

"Oh, great!" Garfield grumbled, climbing up onto Odie's back to avoid the bugs. "I haven't felt this happy since the vet dewormed me!"

"Well, at least we're in," Hairball whispered.

"What now?" Garfield asked.

"You are my prisoners!" boomed an angry voice from down the hall.

Magico, the evil wizard, advanced toward the terrified pets. The ancient sorcerer stood more than six feet tall. His long white beard draped down from his wrinkly face. His shining black robe brushed across the floor and seemed to be made of smoke or liquid instead of cloth. A tall, cone-shaped hat rested on his head. His eyes glowed red with wicked magic.

Garfield looked the mighty wizard over. There was no denying it. This was one really, really bad dude! Garfield pulled his shoulders back, sucked his

belly in, and screamed, "Run!"

With Hairball hiding in Odie's fur, the three pets bolted away from the wizard. They dashed through a series of twisting, curving hallways, turning right, then left, then right again. Each time they paused, the sound of the wizard's footsteps grew louder.

"He's following us!" Hairball cried.

"Great," Garfield moaned. "Maybe *he* knows where we're going. Because obviously *you* don't!"

The group stopped in front of a solid wooden door.

"In here!" Hairball instructed.

Garfield hesitated. "Are you sure? What if there's something more creepy than old red-eyes in there?"

Magico's footsteps drew nearer.

"Would you rather stay here and face him?" Hairball asked.

"Good point," Garfield replied. "In we go!"

The fat cat threw open the heavy wooden door, and the trio stepped inside —right into the wizard's laboratory!

"Well, we've saved Magico a lot of trouble by running right to where he wants us," Garfield said sarcastically. "Wouldn't want to wear the old man out by making him chase us all over the fortress."

Hairball looked around and spied a tall bookshelf. "I have a plan," the tiny cat said.

"I *hate* it when he says that!" Garfield groaned.

"We'll climb up to the top of that bookcase," Hairball continued. "See that large statue on the top shelf, Garfield? When Magico comes in, you push it off. It'll conk him on the head and knock him out, and we can rescue the king."

"Oh, I'm sorry, were you talking to me?" Garfield asked lazily. "I stopped listening after I heard the word 'climb.'"

Footsteps echoed in the hall just outside the lab.

"Climb!" Garfield shouted. Huffing and puffing all the way to the top, he scrambled up the bookcase with Odie right behind him.

Garfield stood behind the heavy troll statue. "Probably one of old red-eye's close relatives," he guessed.

Hairball, meanwhile, had found an ancient book of spells up on the shelf. He pushed open the dusty book, which was bigger than he was, and began to read.

"*How to switch the heads on two different people or animals,*" he read.

Garfield looked at Odie. "What a terrifying thought," he said.

"*How to make people or animals*

*tiny*," Hairball continued reading. "Hey! That's the one he used on me. But I don't see any instructions on how to reverse it. Let's see. This one says *How to make a single bowl of soup feed ten people*."

"I wonder if that would work on lasagna?" Garfield muttered.

"Wait a minute," Hairball said, reading as fast as he could. "This is interesting. Here's a section on how to defeat the wizard's power."

"That's what we need!" Garfield exclaimed. "What does it say? And does it say if that soup spell works on lasagna?"

Before Hairball could answer, the door to the lab burst open and in walked the wizard.

"Get ready," whispered Hairball. "Now!"

Garfield shoved the troll statue off the top shelf. It hurtled down toward the wizard but passed right through him, as if he were a ghost. The statue crashed onto the floor, and the wizard disappeared.

"Good plan," said a voice from the shadows. "But that was not the real me. Here I am." Magico stepped from a dark

corner of the lab. His burning red eyes stared up at the pets. "That was only a projection of my image. A good trick, don't you think? Gets them every time!"

The wizard waved his wrinkled hand in a wide circle. Magically, a hole opened in the wall behind the pets.

"Something tells me that's not the shortcut to the cafeteria," Garfield said, looking at the opening behind them.

Magico pointed a bony finger at the trio. A blast of purple magic shot from his fingertips, knocking the pets into the hole.

"Ahhhhhhh!" Garfield yelled as he tumbled down a dark tunnel with his eyes squeezed firmly shut. Suddenly, he stopped moving. When he opened his eyes again, Garfield saw that he and Odie were sitting on the stone floor of the wizard's dungeon. Their arms were tied behind their backs. The room was lit by only a few torches on the walls.

"And just when I thought things couldn't get any worse," Garfield said, "surprise! They got worse!" He looked over at Odie, who was battling to loosen his ropes. His left ear itched, and he couldn't move his paw to scratch it.

Hairball popped out from under Odie's ear. "Sorry about the itch, Odie, old pal," Hairball said, scratching the spot. "I grabbed on to you when we started falling."

"There you are!" cried Garfield. "I wondered where our brave leader had run off to."

"Well, I had to hang on to Odie," Hairball explained. "If you had landed on me, I would have been squashed as flat as a penny."

A weak voice whispered in the darkness. "Hairball? Is that you?"

Hairball scooted over the top of Odie's head and peered into the black shadows. There sat King Butterball, all tied up like Garfield and Odie. "Your Majesty!" Hairball shouted excitedly. "I've found you!"

"Hairball, my loyal friend," said the king weakly. "You've brought help to rescue me."

"These are my two new friends, Garfield and Odie," Hairball explained, pointing at the pets. "And this is His Majesty, King Butterball."

"Nice to meet you, King," said Garfield. "As you can see, I'm about as good at rescuing as I am at dieting."

"Don't worry," said Hairball. "I'll have all of you untied in a jiffy." He went to work, quickly untying Garfield, then Odie, and finally the king. "Come on. We're getting out of here."

Riding atop Odie's head, Hairball led the others up a winding staircase.

"Whatever happens from now on, at least we learned that Odie's head is good for something besides making buckets of drool," Garfield said as he

scrambled up the curving staircase.

At the top of the stairs was a thick wooden door. "I'll just slip through the keyhole and unlock the door," Hairball suggested. With that, he disappeared into the tiny opening. A moment later, the king and the pets heard a *click*. "Got it!" Hairball called through the keyhole.

Just then, an angry voice came from the other side of the door. "You!" the voice boomed.

It was Magico.

"I thought I'd seen the last of you when I shrunk you down to mouse-size," the wizard raged. "So you decided you'd sneak down into my dungeon!"

Peering through the keyhole, Garfield saw Magico grasp Hairball firmly in his gnarled, bony hand.

"I suppose you thought you could rescue the king," Magico said. "Well, I

have other plans for you . . . in my lab!"
The wizard stormed off.

"Did you hear that?" asked the
king in a panic when Magico had gone.
"He's taking Hairball to his lab. Who
knows what horrible spells he'll cast on
my poor cat. What shall we do?"

"I vote for a large lunch followed
by a long nap!" Garfield said hopefully.

"There's only one thing to do," the
king continued, straightening his royal
robes. "Hairball came to rescue me, and
now I'm going to rescue him!"

"So, then, nobody else votes for
lunch and a nap?" Garfield asked. "I'm
just double-checking."

"And you are going to help me!" the
king commanded Garfield in his most
regal tone.

"I knew he was going to say that,"
Garfield moaned to Odie.

King Butterball, Garfield, and Odie slipped out of the dark dungeon and quietly made their way toward Magico's lab.

"Are we going to waltz right into the lab and say, 'Give up your evil ways, you bad wizard, and give us back our friend?'" Garfield asked. His panic was growing as each step brought them closer to the lab. "Or maybe we should say, 'Hey, Magico, it's time for your favorite TV shows down in the dungeon. You wouldn't want to miss *Who Wants to Be a Wizard?* or *110 Fast and Easy Recipes Using the*

*Brains of Small Lizards!*'"

"I have an idea," the king declared. "You two create a distraction to draw Magico from his lab. Then I'll sneak in and grab Hairball, and we'll all run away."

"Well, I can certainly see why you're the leader of this great land," Garfield said sarcastically. "With ideas like that, it's amazing your entire kingdom hasn't been turned into a giant Whoopee Burger drive-in restaurant. Which, now that I mention it, doesn't sound like a bad idea. But since I don't have a better plan—I'm pretty new to this whole rescue thing—I guess yours will have to do."

The three would-be heroes tiptoed up to the door to the evil wizard's lab. King Butterball pointed down the hall to a large suit of armor. Garfield got the idea. Odie, of course, did not, but he

followed Garfield in his usual oblivious
state. The king hid in a small alcove
near the lab's entrance, then he nodded
at Garfield.

The fat cat pushed and pushed against the heavy suit of armor, but he couldn't budge it. "I need a little help here, Odie," he whined. "Just pretend that this armor is a large, juicy T-bone steak. Yumm!"

Odie began to drool. The image of the armor transformed in his mind into a seven-foot-tall steak. He leaped up to take a bite and sent the armor tumbling to the ground.

*CRASH!*

The heavy suit of armor slammed into the stone floor. Garfield and Odie didn't wait to see what would happen next—they took off down the hall as fast as their paws would carry them.

The door to Magico's lab flew open, and out stormed the wizard. "Who dares disturb the great Magico?" he raged. Flames leaped from his eyes and smoke poured from his ears when he spotted the overturned armor. With an angry growl, he raced down the hall in search of the intruders.

The king sprang from his hiding place and dashed into the lab. He spotted Hairball, who was trapped inside a crystal ball that rested on a counter.

"Your Majesty!" Hairball shouted, his voice muffled by the thick crystal surrounding him. "I know how to defeat the wizard. I found the secret in his book of magic spells." Hairball pointed to the wizard's bookcase. "The book says we must find a way to turn Magico's power against him," Hairball explained.

"Well, well, well," boomed a voice from behind the king. "Isn't this cozy?" Magico stepped into the lab clutching Garfield in one hand, Odie in the other. "All of the heroes, together in one place."

"Hey, King," Garfield panted as he dangled helplessly from the wizard's fist. "The running away part. That part didn't work!"

Magico dropped Garfield and Odie onto the floor. "And now, I shall give you a small demonstration of my power!" the evil wizard snarled.

"Could we take a raincheck on the demonstration?" Garfield suggested. "Let's just wait for the cable TV special *Magico's Wicked World of Power*. Catchy, don't you think?"

Magico raised his hands above his head and began chanting:

*"Oh, magic in purples*
*And power in reds,*
*Take these two creatures*
*And flip-flop their heads!"*

Red and purple smoke filled the lab. When the smoke cleared, Garfield's head was on Odie's body, and Odie's head was on Garfield's body.

Garfield looked down at his new dog body and shrieked. "Ahhh! I'm a dog!

You turned me into a dog! Your evil knows no bounds!"

Odie, meanwhile, stared down at his furry orange gut. Patting the big belly, he let out a moan.

"Oh, don't think *you* got the worst of this, Odie!" Garfield ranted. "You've been upgraded to a cat. But I'm a—a— I can't bear to say it again!"

Odie looked up and saw Hairball

trapped inside the crystal ball. He had grown fond of the tiny cat during their adventures together. Of course, the week before, he had grown fond of a lump of moldy cheese, but Odie really did like Hairball.

The puppy turned to dash across the lab to help his friend, but since he was now using Garfield's body, the dash was more of a crawl. Still, he moved as fast as his fat furry legs would take him.

"Stop!" Magico shouted. "Or I will destroy you!"

But Odie didn't stop. He reached the crystal ball and gave it a big, slobber-filled lick—at the same moment the evil wizard fired a magical blast from his fingertips. Odie's tongue knocked the crystal ball into the edge of a stone shelf. The ball split in half, freeing Hairball. He dived out of the way just as the flaming magic blast struck the empty crystal ball.

The magical burst entered the top of one of the crystal ball's halves. The powerful energy slid along the smooth glass surface, then shot out from the bottom of the crystal ball, heading right back at Magico!

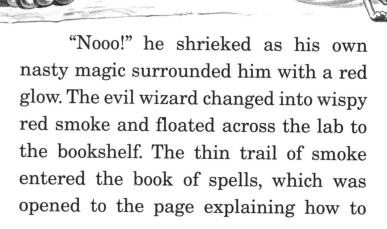

"Nooo!" he shrieked as his own nasty magic surrounded him with a red glow. The evil wizard changed into wispy red smoke and floated across the lab to the bookshelf. The thin trail of smoke entered the book of spells, which was opened to the page explaining how to

defeat a wizard. The book slammed shut with a loud thud, trapping Magico inside.

With the wizard gone, all his evil magic reversed itself.

*FLASH!*

In an instant, Garfield's and Odie's

heads switched back to their own bodies.

Garfield threw his arms around Odie. "I never thought I'd be so happy to see that ugly head on that ugly body," the fat cat cried as he patted Odie on the back.

*POP!*

Hairball expanded to his normal size. "Hey, cat!" he said, stepping up to Garfield. "I'm taller than you! Glad I'm not wider."

Hairball jumped happily into King Butterball's arms and began to purr.

"Thank you all for rescuing me!" exclaimed the king.

Outside the wizard's fortress, the dark skies brightened. The king's brave knights awakened from the evil spell that had kept them frozen. One knight looked down at his empty hand and growled. "Hey!" he yelled. "Who took my chicken leg?!"

Garfield, Odie, Hairball, and King Butterball traveled back to the good king's castle. There, they were met by a cheering crowd of the king's subjects, happy for his return.

"So how do we get home?" Garfield asked Hairball. "Do we have to chant some dopey chant? Click our heels together? Say some magic words?"

"No, none of that stuff," Hairball replied, remembering his end of the bargain. "All you have to do is dive into the moat. When you resurface, you'll be back in your world."

"Not another dunking?" Garfield asked. "Isn't there a drier way?"

"Thank you again!" said the king, waving good-bye.

Garfield and Hairball shook paws. "The next time you need me to save someone, make sure it's a pizza delivery guy!" Garfield said. Then he and Odie dived into the moat.

The two pets resurfaced a moment later and climbed onto shore. They were back at the Medieval Festival. Jon came rushing over to them.

"There you two are!" he shouted. "Where have you been? I've been looking all over for you. We have to hurry."

"Don't tell me," Garfield grumbled. "Another round of jousting, right?"

"There's an old guy dressed like a wizard," Jon explained. "He's about to begin a magic show!"

"A wizard doing magic?" Garfield exclaimed, turning to run away. "That's my cue to disappear!"

## About Garfield's Creator

**Jim Davis** was born in Marion, Indiana, and was promptly dropped on his head—which could explain his lifelong desire to be a cartoonist. Jim still lives in the Hoosier state, preferring the quiet joys of country life, where a man can walk his pig in peace.

## About the Author

**Michael Teitelbaum** was born in Brooklyn, New York, at a very early age. As a child he loved cartoons, baseball, and the Marx Brothers. As a grown-up he loves cartoons, baseball, and the Marx Brothers, and is lucky enough to have spent over twenty years writing books based on cartoons, baseball, and humor. Michael and his wife, Sheleigah, split their time between New York City and their farmhouse in upstate New York.

## About the Illustrator

**Mike Fentz** flunked flute-a-phone lessons in the fourth grade. Fifth grade gave rise to a new career—doodling cartoons in his textbooks. To this day, he's still doodling cartoons in books.

Mike lives in Muncie, Indiana, with his wife, Anne, his two daughters, Jessica and Rachel, a cat, and a slightly used guinea pig.